2/97

The Berenstain Bears
GROW-IT!

Mother Nature Has Such a Green Thumb

Stan & Jan Berenstain

Random House 🏠 New York

Copyright © 1996 by Berenstain Enterprises, Inc. All rights reserved under International and Pan-American Copyright Conventions. Published in the United States by Random House, Inc., New York, and simultaneously in Canada by Random House of Canada Limited, Toronto. *Library of Congress Cataloging-in-Publication Data:* Berenstain, Stan, 1923– The Berenstain Bears grow-it / Stan & Jan Berenstain. p. cm. — (First time do-it books) SUMMARY: As Brother and Sister help Mama plant seeds in the garden, they discover the importance of seeds and how they become useful and important plants. ISBN 0-679-87315-5 (trade) — ISBN 0-679-97315-X (lib. bdg.) [1. Seeds—Fiction. 2. Plants—Fiction. 3. Gardening—Fiction. 4. Bears—Fiction.] I. Berenstain, Jan, 1923– . II. Title. III. Series: Berenstain, Stan, 1923– First time do-it books. PZ7.B4483Berh 1996 [E]—dc20 96-1842
Printed in the United States of America 10 9 8 7 6 5 4 3 2 1

"Come, cubs," said Mama Bear as she headed out the front door. "Today's the day you promised to help me plant the garden."

"Plant the garden?" said Brother. "I was going to play baseball with Cousin Fred."

"Lizzy and I were planning a party for our dolls," said Sister.

PRESENTING
- PROFESSOR ACTUAL FACTUAL
- DIRECTOR OF THE BEARSONIAN INSTITUTION
- FOREMOST BEAR SCIENTIST OF HIS TIME

PERHAPS BROTHER AND SISTER WILL CHANGE THEIR MINDS WHEN THEY UNDERSTAND HOW IMPORTANT PLANTS ARE. BECAUSE THAT'S THE WORD FOR PLANTS: <u>IMPORTANT!</u>

FROM THE TINIEST BACTERIUM (THAT'S RIGHT, BACTERIA ARE PLANTS)…

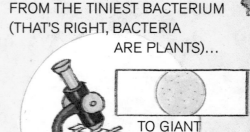

TO GIANT REDWOOD TREES, THE BIGGEST LIVING THINGS ON EARTH…

"A deal's a deal," said Mama. "This way, please."

"It's not fair!" said Brother. "Besides, plants are boring!"

"B-O-R-I-N-G!" added Sister.

...AND ALL THE THOUSANDS OF PLANTS IN BETWEEN, PLANTS ARE I-M-P-O-R-T-A-N-T!

WITHOUT PLANTS, THERE WOULD BE NO OTHER FORM OF LIFE ON EARTH. OUR BEAUTIFUL BLUE-GREEN PLANET WOULD BE JUST ANOTHER DEAD ROCK FLOATING THROUGH SPACE.

"Oh?" said Mama. "Then I guess you think popcorn, chocolate chip cookies, and pancakes with maple syrup are boring, too. Because all those things come from plants."

ALL THE YUMMY THINGS MAMA MENTIONED DO COME FROM PLANTS. CHOCOLATE CHIPS COME FROM THE CACAO PLANT—THE SAME PLANT THAT COCOA COMES FROM. COOKIES AND PANCAKES COME FROM GRAIN PLANTS. MAPLE SYRUP IS THE SAP OF THE SUGAR MAPLE TREE.

IF COCOA COMES FROM THE CACAO PLANT, WHY ISN'T COCOA CALLED CACAO?

HMM, DO YOU HAVE ANY OTHER QUESTIONS?

SOME IMPORTAN

CORN

WHEAT

As Mama spoke, she dug a line of small holes in the flower bed. "Sister, will you please pour a little water in each hole?" As Sister did so, Mama tapped seedlings from their pots and put them in their new homes.

Pouring water wasn't as much fun as having a party for your dolls. But it was fun—sort of.

RAIN PLANTS

RICE

OATS

WE'LL CONSULT OUR EXPERT. OH, FARMER BEN!

YES, PROFESSOR, I HAVE ANOTHER QUESTION: WHY DOES POPCORN POP?

IT'S REALLY VERY SIMPLE. POPCORN IS JUST A THICK-SKINNED CORN. WHEN HEATED, THE MOISTURE INSIDE EXPANDS AND CAUSES IT TO "POP".

POPCORN

"Now, Brother," said Mama, "when the plants are in place, press the soil around each one with your fingers."

It wasn't as much fun as playing baseball. But Brother liked dirt and dirt liked Brother.

POPCORN AND ICE CREAM ARE THE LEAST OF IT. WE GET ALL OUR FOOD FROM PLANTS...

OR FROM ANIMALS WHO GET THEIR FOOD FROM PLANTS.

MUCH OF OUR CLOTHING IS MADE OF COTTON WHICH IS A PLANT.

"Nor are ice cream and honey very boring," said Mama.

"But they don't come from plants," said Brother.

"They come from cows and honeybees," said Sister.

"Ah, yes!" said Mama. "But cows make their milk and cream from the plants they eat, and bees make their honey from the nectar they get from plants."

INCLUDING MY SHIRT AND PANTS.

AND MY BLOUSE AND JUMPER.

MANY OF OUR

HOUSES

AND MUCH OF OUR

FURNITURE

OUR HOUSE IS A TREE.

ARE MADE OF WOOD. WE GET WOOD FROM TREES, AND TREES ARE PLANTS.

"Well, we have lots more to do," said Mama. "Brother, run up and get the bag and the shopping list on the kitchen table while I get the shopping cart."

MOST PAPER COMES FROM WOOD. EVERY BOOK YOU'VE EVER READ—INCLUDING THIS ONE—COMES FROM PLANTS.

The Berenstain Bears
GROW-IT!
Mother Nature Has Such a Green Thumb!

WELL, IF YOU'LL EXCUSE US, PROFESSOR, WE HAVE TO GET BACK AND HELP MAMA WITH THE GARDEN.

BUT I HAVEN'T YET TOLD YOU THE MOST IM-PORTANT THING WE GET FROM PLANTS: **THE BREATH OF LIFE!**

"Where are we going?" asked Sister.

"To Farmer Ben's Produce and Garden Supply Shop, just down the road," said Mama.

THE BREATH OF LIFE?

THAT'S RIGHT. PLANTS HELP MAKE THE AIR WE BREATHE. HERE'S A LITTLE RHYME ABOUT IT.

Plants make a gas
called OXYGEN,
the gas we use
when we breathe IN.

Plants need a gas
called CO_2—
which they get
from me and you.
We breathe OUT CO_2!

That's something
we can think about
as we are breathing
in and out.

Brother found the bag and the list.

WHILE PLANTS ARE MORE IMPORTANT TO US THAN WE ARE TO THEM, THERE ARE WAYS WE CAN HELP THEM. LET'S SEE HOW THE THINGS ON MAMA'S LIST CAN HELP PLANTS.

1. SEEDS

PLANTING SEEDS DOES MORE THAN HELP THEM. IT GIVES THEM A CHANCE AT LIFE.

2. VERMICULITE

THIS IS A SPECIAL MINERAL THAT IS SO GOOD AT HOLDING WATER THAT IT'S AN EXCELLENT SEED STARTER.

This is what the
list looked like.

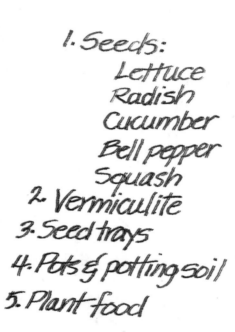

1. Seeds:
    Lettuce
    Radish
    Cucumber
    Bell pepper
    Squash
2. Vermiculite
3. Seed trays
4. Pots & potting soil
5. Plant food

3. SEED TRAYS

WHEN SEEDS SPROUT, THEY ARE CALLED SEEDLINGS. SMALL ONES DON'T MIND CROWDS.

4. POTS AND POTTING SOIL

AFTER A WHILE, SEEDLINGS NEED TO BE GENTLY SEPARATED AND GIVEN HOMES OF THEIR OWN.

5. PLANT FOOD

THE PROPER AMOUNT OF PLANT FOOD HELPS NOURISH PLANTS. BUT READ THE DIRECTIONS CAREFULLY. JUST AS TOO MUCH FOOD IS NOT GOOD FOR US, TOO MUCH FOOD CAN HARM PLANTS.

"What's in the bag, Mama?" asked Brother.
"Papa's lunch," she said. "We're going to cu[t]
through the woods on the way to Farmer
Ben's and take Papa his lunch."

OF COURSE,
MOTHER NATURE DOESN'T
HAVE TO BUY SEEDS
AT FARMER BEN'S.
SHE MAKES ZILLIONS AND
ZILLIONS OF THEM.

SOME ARE
SMALLER THAN
THIS DOT.

SOME, LIKE THE
COCONUT, ARE VERY
LARGE. (IT'S NATURE'S
LARGEST SEED.)

MAPLE SEEDS MAKE
A MUSTACHE…

OR A RHINO
HORN.

"Mama," said Brother. "How come Mother Nature doesn't have to go to the garden supply store and buy stuff like potting soil, plant food, and vermiculite—whatever that is—and we do?"

MOTHER NATURE CERTAINLY DOES HAVE A GREEN THUMB. BUT THAT DOESN'T MEAN SHE DOESN'T NEED HELP AND PROTECTION FROM TIME TO TIME AND PLACE TO PLACE.

AMONG THE PLACES THAT NEED PROTECTION ARE THE GREAT RAIN FORESTS. THEY ARE VERY VALUABLE.

THEY PRODUCE HUGE AMOUNTS OF OXYGEN FOR THE ATMOSPHERE.

"Because," said Mama with a smile, "Mother Nature is a much better gardener than I am."

THEY PROVIDE FOOD AND HOMES FOR THOUSANDS OF FORMS OF ANIMAL LIFE.

HI, THERE!

SOME IMPORTANT MEDICINES COME FROM PLANTS. MANY MORE MAY BE DISCOVERED.

Papa was glad to see Mama and the cubs. He was especially glad to see his lunch.

Farmer Ben was glad to see them, too. Not only were they good customers, they were friends and neighbors as well.

FARMER BEN'S PRODUCE AND GARDEN SUPPLY SHOP

IN THE LANGUAGE OF SCIENCE, A PLACE LIKE A RAIN FOREST IS CALLED AN ECOSYSTEM.

AN ECO-WHAT?

THE WORD COMES FROM "ECOLOGY." IT MEANS A PLACE WHERE ALL THE PARTS OF NATURE ARE IN BALANCE. THERE ARE DIFFERENT KINDS OF ECOSYSTEMS. THEY ALL NEED TO BE PROTECTED.

FOREST SYSTEMS NEED TO BE PROTECTED:

THIS

NOT THIS

WATER SYSTEMS NEED TO BE PROTECTED FROM POLLUTION.

After buying the things on her list, Mama bought some of Ben's fresh produce. She bought beets, peas, carrots, and yams. "Ben's roadside shop is kind of interesting," she said as they headed home.

"Yes, kind of," said Brother.

"Wow!" Sister said. "All those different kinds of seeds!"

DESERT SYSTEMS, WHERE THE WEB OF LIFE IS STRETCHED THIN, NEED TO BE PROTECTED FROM DAMAGING USE.

THE FOREST, WHERE PAPA DOES HIS WORK, IS AN ECOSYSTEM. PAPA IS PROTECTING IT BY PLANTING TREES TO REPLACE THOSE HE HAS CUT.

"It might be fun if we could grow food like Farmer Ben does," said Sister.

"I'm glad you think so," said Mama. "Because that's exactly what we're going to do!"

HOW TO TURN YOUR HOME INTO AN ECOSYSTEM

BROTHER AND SISTER CHOSE TO START CARROT, BEET, YAM, LETTUCE, AND PEA PLANTS. THESE ARE GOOD CHOICES. BUT THERE ARE MANY OTHER CANDIDATES FOR YOUR HOME-GROWN ECOSYSTEM.

YOU MAY FIND THEM IN… YOUR VEGETABLE BINS,

POTATO BEET

PUMPKIN SQU

CA

And that's what happened that very afternoon. They started carrot, beet, and yam plants in water. And they planted lettuce and peas with a mixture of vermiculite and potting soil in pots and seed trays.

YOUR FRUIT BASKET,

APPLE

ORANGE

LEMON

GRAPEFRUIT

PINEAPPLE

PEAR

PEACH

CHERRIES

OR YOUR FRIDGE.

RADISH

PEPPER

AVOCADO

TOMATO

WATER

WHAT TO PLANT AND HOW TO PLANT IT

ANY PLANT CAN BE GROWN FROM A SEED. BUT PLANTS LIKE CARROTS, POTATOES, BEETS, AND OTHERS CAN ALSO BE GROWN FROM THE VEGETABLE ITSELF.

HOW TO START A CARROT PLA

1. ASK A GROWNUP TO CUT OFF THE TOP OF A CARROT.

2. PUT A LAYER OF PEBBLES IN A DISH OR A SHALLOW BOWL.

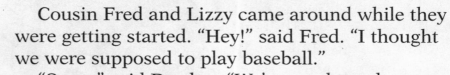

Cousin Fred and Lizzy came around while they were getting started. "Hey!" said Fred. "I thought we were supposed to play baseball."

"Sorry," said Brother. "We're much too busy planting stuff."

"Hey!" said Lizzy. "I thought we were supposed to have a party for our dolls."

"Sorry," said Sister. "We're growing stuff. We're practically going to have our own farm!"

. COVER
HE
EBBLES
ITH WATER.

4. SET CARROT TOP ON PEBBLES.

5. TRANSFER TO POTTING SOIL IN POT WHEN WELL-ROOTED.

6. ADD WATER AND PLANT FOOD— WATCH IT GROW!

YAMS AND OTHER POTATOES MAKE BEAUTIFUL HANGING PLANTS.

And they practically did. Before long, they had plants growing all over the place.

PLANTS CAN BE GROWN FROM SEEDS THAT YOU GET FROM THE DIFFERENT FRUITS YOU EAT: APPLES AND PEARS, ALL CITRUS FRUITS, MELONS AND SQUASHES, AND MORE.

HOW TO PLANT PUMPKIN SEEDS

1. MIX SOME VERMICULITE WITH POTTING SOIL.

2. PUT A TROWELFUL IN A POT WITH A PEBBLE IN THE BOTTOM (TO COVER THE HOLE).

3. SINK THREE SEEDS POINTY END UP, HALFWAY INTO SOIL.

5. PUT IN A DARK PLACE UNTIL THE SEEDS SPROUT (ABOUT A WEEK).

6. ADD POTTING SOIL TO COVER THE SEEDS. SOAK WITH WATER AND PLANT FOOD. PUT IN THE SUN.

. SPRINKLE WITH ATER UNTIL A TTLE OF IT LEAKS UT THE BOTTOM.

PUMPKIN, SQUASH, AND MELON PLANTS ARE VINES WITH BLOSSOMS.

ALL THE OTHER FRUITS BECOME SHRUBS AND TREES, WHICH ALSO BLOSSOM— EVENTUALLY.

In fact, the Bears' living room was starting to look like a jungle!

MOTHER NATURE CERTAINLY DOES HAVE A GREEN THUMB. BUT YOU KNOW WHAT? SO DO WE!

QUESTION: HOW DID PROFESSOR ACTUAL FACTUAL LEARN SO MUCH ABOUT MOTHER NATURE'S GREEN THUMB?

ANSWER: BY GOING ON FIELD TRIPS AND INTERVIEWING OTHER EXPERTS.

IT'S A JUNGLE IN HERE!